LIBRARIAN

READING SKILLS A PLUS.

LIZARD FARMER

STRIKE IT RICH!
SEND AWAY FOR YOUR
LIZARD-FARM STARTER
KIT TODAY!

AND RECEIVE A FREE
COPY OF
LIZARDICIOUS
100 RECIPES FOR
THE NEW CHICKEN.

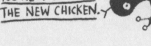

SUBSTITUTE TEACHER NEEDED TO TAKE
OVER FOR THE SUBSTITUTE TEACHER
WHO TOOK OVER FOR THE SUBSTITUTE
TEACHER SUBSTITUTING FOR THE
SUBSTITUTE TEACHER WHO WAS FILLING
IN FOR MRS. BEASLEY, WHO IS
OUT WITH A NERVOUS BREAKDOWN.

PAINTER

LOOKING FOR THE NEXT VAN GOGH
TO PAINT PINE VILLAGE CONDOMINIUMS.

WAITRESS

GLAMOUR AWAITS YOU IN AN
EXCITING CAREER AS A TABLE-
WAITING SPECIALIST.
APPLY AT DOOLEY'S DINER.

POET

DESPERATELY SEEKING TALENTED
POET TO FIND A WORD THAT RHYMES
WITH BIRD.

STORY TELLER

PERSON NEEDED TO TURN
ORDINARY WORDS LIKE KITE
AND SHOE AND TREE AND
NEAT INTO MAGICAL
TALES
OF
ADVENTURE
AND
WONDER.

ZOOKEEPER

PLEASE NO INQUIRIES REGARDING
REASON FOR PREVIOUS ZOOKEEPER'S
DEPARTURE (OR X-RAY OF
TIGER'S ABDOMEN).

Nana
CRACKS THE CASE!

nana
CRACKS THE CASE!

By Kathleen Lane
Concept by Cabell Harris
Illustrated by Sarah Horne

chronicle books · san francisco

To my Nana, Selma Letitia Schumann, and my children's Nana,
Shirley Schumann Harris. Between them they have provided
a lifetime supply of stories.
— C. H. —

For Leo and John Kentucky.
— K. L. —

For the Geese, with my love. I've never known so much fuss!
— S. H. —

Text © 2009 by Cabell Harris and Kathleen Lane.
Illustrations © 2009 by Sarah Horne.

Wikki Stix is a trademark of Omnicor, Inc.

Book design by Eloise Leigh.
Typeset in Plantin.
The illustrations in this book were rendered in ink.
Manufactured in China.

Library of Congress Cataloging-in-Publication Data
Lane, Kathleen, 1967–
  Nana cracks the case! / concept by Cabell Harris ; written by Kathleen
Lane ; illustrated by Sarah Horne.
      p. cm.
  Summary: Eufala and Bog's very feisty grandmother takes a job with the
Crispy County Police Department, searching for a candy thief.
  ISBN 978-0-8118-6258-5
  [1. Grandmothers—Fiction. 2. Candy—Fiction.] I. Harris, Cabell.
II. Horne, Sarah, 1979– ill. III. Title.
  PZ7.L2501Nan 2009
  [Fic]—dc22
  2007037929

10 9 8 7 6 5 4 3 2 1

Chronicle Books LLC
680 Second Street, San Francisco, California 94107

www.chroniclekids.com

Chapters

Can You Keep a Secret?

Nana held her newspaper up close to her face, just to be certain that the ad did indeed say wigs and not pigs, which she was clean out of at the moment.

"Well, that settles it then," said Nana, folding her newspaper back into a rectangle and tossing it down onto her now not-so-puffy cream puff. "I am the perfect candidate for the job."

It did seem that Nana had all of the qualifications necessary to be a detective. Not only did she own the various wigs mentioned in the ad, "but," said Nana, "I must admit that I can also, when necessary, be a bit sneaky."

Nana did not often admit to being sneaky. In fact, you might want to turn down the corner on this page, as it will probably be the last page on which Nana ever admits to being sneaky again.

Of course, it would be very hard for Nana to deny her sneakiness with the evidence sitting right there on her kitchen table for all to see.

Surely you've already noticed it. Right next to the Fudge Freezie wrapper. No, not that Fudge Freezie wrapper, the other one.

Yes, that's it. *The Joy of Napping.*

It doesn't look very sneaky, no, that is true. In fact, now that you have found it on Nana's table, you might be a little disappointed. Napping? you might say. I am not interested in

napping. I prefer much more exciting things, like tetherball.

But that's just it, you see. Nana is not interested in napping either. And that is precisely why she has on her table a book called *The Joy of Napping*.

Well that makes no sense whatsoever you must be thinking. And quite right you are. But that is only because you do not yet—not for several more sentences still—know the secret. It's not a very big secret, nothing on the scale and grandeur of, say, turning your backyard into a rice paddy, or hiding a 40-pound reptile inside your closet. Now those sorts of secrets, as Eufala and Bog can tell you, require a fair amount of sneakiness to keep.

Oh dear, you haven't yet met Eufala and Bog, have you? What a lot we have to cover.

Well, in addition to being Nana's grand-children, Eufala and Bog happen to be the only two people on earth who know the secret. They have not even told their own mother the secret, nor will they ever. Not because Nana has asked that they not tell their mother—this would be deceitful, of course—but because they are children, and children, unlike adults, know a great many things without having to be told. And so Eufala and Bog know, they just know, that they are to never speak a word of it.

So here it is then, the se-cret: Book covers, you see, are quite removable. Not only that, but they are quite swappable, quite switch-aroundable, if you will.

One might, for example, have in one's house—or more specifically, on one's kitchen table—a book about some-thing very fascinating, such as  tightrope walking. But the cover on this book might say something completely different and not fascinating at all.

The Joy of Napping, for example.

Why do such a thing? Why not leave books and covers as they are? Well, in Nana's case the answer is simple, and her name is Elaine. Elaine is Nana's daughter, mother of Eufala and Bog, and the very worst kind of worrier. Not at all the sort of person who would be comfortable with the career choices Nana has made.

Elaine would not like, for example, that her mother was recently employed as a deep-sea fisherman, and even more recently as a hockey referee, and even more recently than that—last week, in fact—as a backhoe operator. This is someone who moves great piles of dirt around and who must never—as Nana learned on her last day of work—read the newspaper while driving. Because it is very easy, as Nana learned—quite simple, really—to move a great pile of dirt onto something that should not have a great pile of dirt on top of it. Because

that something can sometimes be a someone, and that someone can sometimes be something of a complainer. But no matter, Mrs. Poutabout was completely unharmed and, what's more, with the money she received from Muck Movers for her inconvenience (countless beauty appointments to pluck pebbles from her hair) was able to remodel her kitchen, which she had been

wanting to do for years and which came out quite lovely, as Nana saw for herself when Mrs. Poutabout invited her over one afternoon for pie and tea.

And oh yes, the point. The point is, if Elaine knew that Nana was carrying on as she was carrying on—two of Elaine's favorite words are *carrying* and *on*—she would not be at all happy about it. So very not at all happy that she might insist Nana move into that hideous place where

HMMPH...

she works, that place for old people, where there would be no more *carrying* or *on*, only *sitting* and *around*. Because nanas, you see, are not supposed to carry on.

Nanas are supposed to get scowly looks on their faces and wear cloppy shoes and drink their prune juice and be mindful of anything slippery. They are not supposed to

become backhoe operators or marine biologists or circus performers (actually Nana did not *join* the circus, she only substituted while the trapeze artist recovered from a broken leg). And they must never—because they are so very fragile, you see—become detectives.

And now you understand the reason that

Nana must always keep *The Joy of Napping* on her table, so that whenever Elaine drops by for a visit, she will see that Nana is being a very good and proper old person. *Good* and *proper* are two other words that Elaine is very fond of.

"Now then," said Nana, "no time like the present to become a detective." And with that she grabbed her coat from its hook and was out the door.

Mustn't Forget to Bring Along a Wig

Oh dear, she nearly forgot the most important thing. Nana hurried back inside her house and into her bedroom and over to her dresser where she keeps her tops—that is to say, anything having to do with the top half of her. Everything organized in the proper order, of course. Shirts and sweaters (the bottommost of tops) in the bottom drawer. Next up, scarves. Followed, in the next drawer up, by teeth. And in the top drawer, the toppest of tops, her wigs. Her many, many—many, many, many—wigs.

If some extremely bored person were to count up all of the wigs in Crispy County, not

that anyone would ever do such a thing—it would be a rather peculiar thing to do—she would likely find that nobody owned a more impressive collection of wigs than Nana.

Nana opened up the top drawer of her dresser and pushed this wig that way, and that wig this way, until she came to just the one.

"Yes, you ought to do," she said to the poofy orange and black-spotted wig, one of her very favorites, and after pushing the poof into her purse, she was once again out the door, down

the street, over the bridge, across Paprika Street, under the highway, into the mall, past the pet shop, around a stroller, into the ladies' room…*No, no, that's not right*, thought Nana, and she was out the ladies' room, around the stroller, past the pet shop, out the mall, under the highway, into the park, over the bridge, around the corner to the—*Now where on earth did they move the*—Ah, there we go, the Crispy County Police Department.

No Telling What Might Happen

Not far from the police station, in a narrow house on the corner of Honey and Mustard streets, Eufala and Bog sat slouched over their cereal bowls, trying very hard to swallow the last of their oatmeal, the oatmeal that the one-half teaspoon of sugar allowed by their mother had not reached.

While the children picked and pushed at the mush in their bowls, their eyes followed their mother, who was pacing back and forth in front of them, as she often did—so often, in fact, that there was a sunken place in the floor that ran in a triangle from sink to stove to table and back again. What to do with the children while she went to work. This was Elaine's newest worry. *Oh why*, thought Elaine, *did they insist on letting children out of school for an entire summer when a week would be more than sufficient?*

She had just dismissed babysitter number thirty-seven because the careless girl had left a pair of scissors on the floor, where it might have cut off a toe—where it might have cut off an entire foot—had Elaine not returned home in time. And Nana, well, Nana was entirely too old to watch the children for an entire day. There was no telling what might happen.

No telling what might happen was something that Elaine happened to know a thing or two about. It was only five years ago this summer that her husband, Earl—Eufala and Bog's father—had been snatched from the streets of Lettuceburg by an escaped orangutan, who had then hopped the two-o'clock train out of town, Earl flopped over his shoulder like a cheap

carry-on. And away they had gone, never to be seen again—except for a mysterious card that arrived every Christmas from Borneo, wishing the family a very happy holiday season.

"What to do?" muttered Elaine, chewing on the inside of her cheek as if it were a stale stick of bubble gum. "What to do?" from sink to table. "What to do?" from stove to sink. "What to do?" until Eufala finally said, in her most darling voice, "Maybe we can look after ourselves?" And Bog, in a voice so sweet he sounded just like a baby bird, "Yeah, we can do it."

Oh goodness, what well-behaved children.

Slightest Hint of a smile.

Now, before you start choking on your toast or throwing your eggs against the wall and demanding a more exciting book, you might just take a closer look at our two well-behaved children. Of particular interest would be Bog's mouth.

Also worth noting is Eufala's forehead. Yes go ahead and take a peek, we'll wait.

"I can make us lunch," suggested Eufala, her words dripping with honey.

"I'll clip my toenails," chirped Bog—an odd sort of offer, yes, but for months now he had been putting off the task, much to the exasperation of his mother.

"What to do?" This was all their mother had to say in response. As if she hadn't heard them at all. "What to do? What to do?" while Eufala sculpted her oatmeal into a fairy, complete with locks and wings, and Bog turned his into a frog so convincing that a nearby fly took to the ceiling for safety. "What to do? What to do?" for another twenty minutes, until only one *what-to-do* remained.

Beads of... Sweat, from working out just what to say to get her mother to leave...

The Ultimate YOU MUSTN'T

Elaine's only choice—unless she wanted to get fired from her job and subject the family to a life of squalor and starvation—was to leave the children home alone for the day.

And so, after approximately thirty-five sentences that began with *you mustn't* and another fifty-two that began with *be sure to* and *be careful not to,* Elaine locked the children inside the house and headed to work.

Two seconds later, or perhaps not even so long as that, Eufala and Bog plopped down their spoons, hopped from their seats, and were off searching the house for which of the *you-mustn't*s and *you-shouldn't*s they would try today.

It isn't that they are bad children—well, there is quite a lot of evidence to suggest that they are a bit on the mischievous side—but it's hardly as if they set out to be mischievous. Have you ever walked into a room and declared, "I think I shall go make some mischief now"? No, it is far more likely that you set out to invent and create and experiment and explore—all very bright and noble endeavors.

And so if the children's experiments sometimes required the use of their mother's favorite tube of lipstick, it was only because they needed that color red. And if their explorations occasionally ended at the police station, it was only because they wanted to see what the grass would look like spray-painted orange. How could they have possibly guessed that the wind would suddenly pick up, or that Mr. Crossley would cause such a scene over a harmless little

stripe on his necktie?—at least it matched his stripey suit. And if their creations once or twice caused a tiny shriek or two—not everyone is going to find an earwig catapult interesting— well, it was only in the name of invention, without which, anyone would have to admit, the world would be a very uninteresting place. Sir Isaac Newton himself surely caused a shriek or two in his day. And Einstein, well, perhaps not shrieking, but most certainly gasping.

Oh dear, we are getting a bit off track, aren't we? Well then, back we go to the children, who have by now opened half the drawers in the house, plugged in three quarters of the appliances, and just at this very moment are passing each other in the living room and shrugging at each other because, so far anyway, neither has come up with anything worthwhile to do.

Bog picked up his mother's curling iron but was not feeling in the mood for curling the curtains today. Eufala had no sooner plugged in the waffle iron than she had already grown bored of it. Nothing, not even the knife drawer they were to never open, not even the radiator they  were to never go near, not even their favorite game of boiling toiletries in their mother's saucepan, seemed at all interesting.

 There was only one *you-mustn't* left. The ultimate *you-mustn't*. The *you-mustn't*

that their mother always added several exclamation points to the end of whenever she said it. The front door.

"You must never—*never*—open the front door!!"

And that is why Eufala and Bog did not open the front door. Never in a million years would they have so much as touched the doorknob of the front door.

Anyhow, why open the front door when the kitchen window worked just as well—and, they had found, was much less likely to draw the attention of the neighbors.

But first, as their mother had taught them so well, the children set about preparing themselves for the possibility of anything. They would need money of course—and there were plenty of coins to be found in their mother's coat pockets.

They would also need to bring along something to eat in case they got hungry—a bag of chocolate chips from the pantry should keep them from dying of starvation.

Finally and most importantly, their skateboards, in case…well, the skateboards were really just in case they wanted to have some fun.

"I think that's everything," said Eufala.

"I'll carry the chocolate chips," said Bog.

And out the window they dropped, skateboards first, into their mother's newly planted marigolds below.

Choccy Chips

What Experience Do You Have with Thieves?

"Excuse me, young man," Nana said to a nice young man outside the police station. He was wearing a very attractive suit and in Nana's favorite color, too. "Do you know where we go for the interview?"

But the man only growled. Or maybe it was a grumble.

Either way, he was not going to get very far as a detective with that kind of grammar.

"Okay, Scruffy, move it along," said the policemen to the man in the orange suit, and very good advice it was. That's exactly what Nana needed to do if she was going to be the next selected detected—no, that's not what she wanted to say. The next selective detective. Oh tangles, that wasn't it either. Well, never mind, the important thing was to get there on time.

Nana marched up the steps, through the door, over to the clerk, and said in her most official-sounding voice, "Good morning, I'm Nana, and I want to be a detective."

"Yeah, sure you do," said the clerk. "And I want to be a Barnum and Bailey flying trapeze artist."

"How wonderful!" said Nana. "Although I must say I did find the work to be a bit hard on the fingernails." Nana was about to mention a lotion that works wonders on calluses when the clerk handed her an application and pointed to a chair. "Over there," she said. "Fill it out and bring it back."

N-A-N... Nana was just putting the finishing touches on her first name when the sheriff

Crispy County

POLICE DEPARTMENT

APPLICATION FOR EMPLOYMENT

1. WHAT EXPERIENCE DO YOU HAVE WITH THIEVES?
   _____
   _____

2. ON A SCALE OF 1 TO 10, ARE YOU SMART?
   _____
   _____

3. SOLVE: ON WEDNESDAY MORNING 7 DOUGHNUTS
   (WITH SPRINKLES) WENT MISSING FROM
   DAVY DUNKERS' DOUGHNUT SHOP.
   IF THE SUSPECT LEFT THE SHOP AT 7:30
   AND PAID 25¢ TO RIDE THE BUS,
   HOW MANY DOUGHNUTS COULD HE CONSUME IN
   1 HOUR? _____

4. WHICH OF THE FOLLOWING LOOKS THE MOST SUSPICIOUS?

walked in and said to the clerk, "Any applicants yet for the detective job?"

The clerk motioned with her head over toward Nana.

"Anybody else?" asked the sheriff.

"Nope," said the clerk.

"Anybody from yesterday?"

"Nope."

"What about the day before yesterday?"

"Nope."

"How about the day before the day before yesterday?"

"Nope," said the clerk, "and not the day before the day before the day before either."

The sheriff looked at Nana, then back at the clerk, who shook her head in a *nope* sort of way.

Finally, he walked over to Nana and snatched up her application mid-*A*. "Good enough," he said. "Can you start today? No time for questions, I need a detective right away."

"Do you offer a dental plan?" asked Nana,

but the sheriff just handed her a piece of paper, with not one mention of denture care on it anywhere.

Crispy  County
POLICE DEPARTMENT

- - - - - - - - - - - -

CRIME REPORT

ITEM STOLEN :   Yumdums

BRIEF DESCRIPTION: Brown and delicious

QUANTITY MISSING :   One ENTIRE case

TIME OF DAY :   0900 HRS

SUSPECT :   Sneaky

6

Two Pages on Which Very Little Happens

Nana raced to the scene. But not before stopping home for a quick lunch of chocolate noodle casserole, a peanut butter raisin marsh-mallow sandwich on cinnamon swirl bread, and for dessert, a Fudge Freezie, because one of the most important food groups of all is the -eezie group, and that is why Nana always eats at least three Fudge Freezies a day. Good for the bones, you know.

But right after lunch, and right after reading the paper, and right after her after-lunch stretches, and just as soon as she woke up from her after-stretches nap (Nana can hardly help

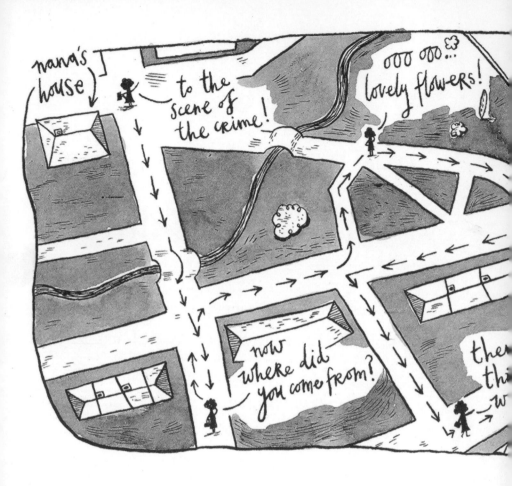

it if lunch and her stretches always make her a little sleepy), it was time to...

Well how about that? She plop forgot. Time for something. Something important.

Oh yes, time to race to the scene!

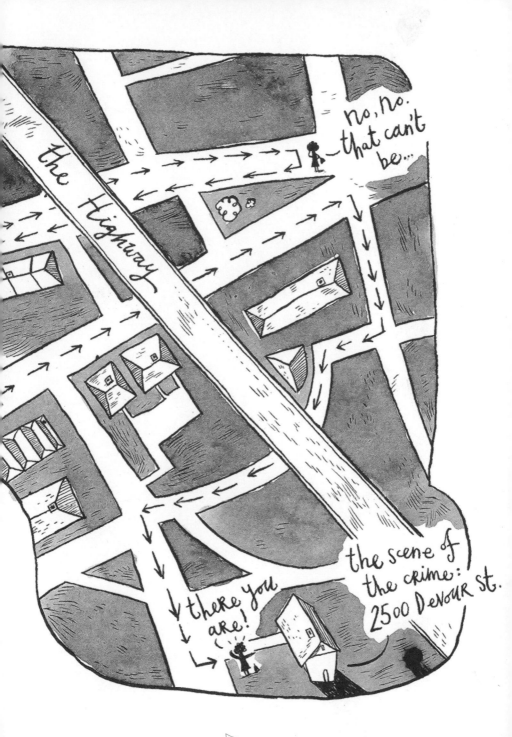

Candy Is Nice but Mischief Is Sweeter

Nothing says fun like CAUTION DO NOT ENTER tape, so when Eufala and Bog arrived in downtown Lettuceberg and saw that yellow ribbon wiggling in the morning breeze, they could hardly get their hands on it fast enough. But other than a bunch of rubble and some grouchy construction workers who told them to scram, there wasn't much to see on the other side.

Pecan Square was just as disappointing. After the children laid out all of the pennies and nickels they had scooped from the fountain, the grand sum was a measly $1.86. That was only enough for three Sugar Squirties and one box of matches, or two cans of Pappy's Flappy Root Beer and six nails, or half a tube of Mighty Glue and eighteen gummy candies.

"Wait!" said Bog, who just remembered the money they had collected from their mother's coat pockets and various other money-finding locations around the house. "Fifty-two cents!"

Together with the $1.86, they now had... $2.38. Plus the $5 bill Eufala had found paper-clipped to some flyer on her mother's desk: "Save the..." somethings—Eufala hadn't read it too closely, but the way she figured it, $5 wasn't going to save much of anything anyway.

"That makes seven dollars and thirty-eight cents," said Eufala.

After shrugging at each other in an okay-I-guess-that-will-have-to-do kind of way, the children evenly divided up the money, then hopped on their skateboards and headed for the Buy-n-Buy.

They had planned to go first to the Buy-n-Buy and then to the park because that was the proper order of things—candy first no matter what—but as they passed by the park, something caught their eye. Not just a single something but multiple somethings. Ducks. All over the place, everywhere you looked, ducks.

With their skateboards kicked up at their sides, the children stared off in the direction of the pond, where some kind of duck rugby match appeared to be getting under way. Every couple of seconds a dinner roll would slide out from underneath a pileup of feathers.

"We should do something," said Bog, his eyes round with excitement.

It was such an obvious statement that Eufala immediately deemed it unworthy of a reply. Instead, without so much as a word, she strode off through the grass, leaving Bog behind in a fit of leaps and skips and "wait-ups!"

Messy, Messy, Messy

A brown house, noted Nana, standing outside the O'Cleary house. Very interesting. Yumdums are brown, too. Says so right here in her...right here in her...right in this handy—now where on earth did she put that crime report?

Well, never mind, she'll just have to find that Yumdum thief without it.

Nana walked in the door, which she measured to be exactly six feet high. *The thief must be somewhere between zero feet and six feet tall,* she wrote in her notebook, where detectives keep all of their most brilliant detectivey thoughts.

Inside the house, what a mess. Wrappers everywhere, all over the floor.

Messy house, noted Nana in her notebook.

In the kitchen, on the counter, next to the sink, behind the black leather glove, in front of the toaster, there was an unfinished glass of milk.

What a waste, wrote Nana in her notebook. *Some cows worked very hard to make that milk.*

Upstairs in the bedroom, on a desk near the window, next to the *How to Steal Stuff* handbook and the smudged-up envelope, there was a bottle of perfume.

Maybe this perfume belongs to the thief, thought Nana. She added this highly important piece of evidence to her list of clues.

"I better get this down to the lab right away," Nana said out loud and rushed outside, straight into a noisy crowd of nosy reporters, all asking questions.

"Who did it?"

"Any clues?"

"What are you going to do to protect our candy supplies?"

"Is it safe to eat chocolate at night?"

But this was no time for answers, Nana had important clues to investigate.

"I'm conducting an important investigation here," she said, "I must ask you all to move aside."

And that is precisely where her bony little elbows pushed them.

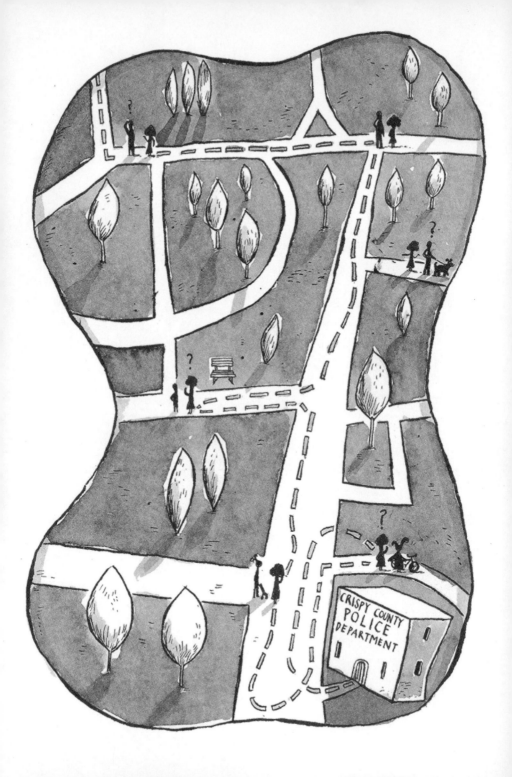

9

Fowl Gone Afoul

The police department was not at all where Nana very clearly remembered leaving it. She had to ask directions from at least twelve people, the last of whom was a five-year-old girl who did not say a word but simply turned herself around and pointed across the street.

"Well, aren't you a sneaky one," said Nana to the large brick building with enormous engraved letters across the top spelling CRISPY COUNTY POLICE DEPARTMENT. "Thought you'd play a little game of hide-and-seek, did you?"

Nana walked up the steps, through the door, and down the hall. She stopped briefly to admire

some very nice black-and-white photography on the wall, then continued on her way, past the clerk's desk and the vending machine and Eufala and Bog and the drinking fountain—

"Eufala! Bog!"

"Nana!"

Now you mustn't interpret those exclamation points to mean anything other than three people who were very happy to see one another. They certainly were not surprised to see one another. It seemed that no matter which way they set off on their adventures, their adventures always had a way of bumping into each other.

Last week when the children were at the Crispy County Arboretum peeling bark off a thousand-year-old giant sequoia for their canoe, there was Nana, leading a group of hikers in a ceremonial blessing of the cocoa tree. The week before, while the children were at the zoo training a peacock to hurdle soda cans—much to the admiration of a large crowd of children—there was Nana, in a zookeeper's jacket, throwing steaks to the monkeys—who, of course, were throwing them right back. In fact, the game of toss might have gone on forever had Eufala and Bog not been there to suggest

to Nana that she might try tossing the steaks to the lions instead.

"Well now," said Nana, "what brings you two down to the police station?"

"I do," said a very grumpy Officer Burly.

He was holding the children's arms, which was a nice enough thing to do; Nana had no objections to walking arm in arm. But it did seem that he was squeezing rather tightly.

That poor Officer Burly, thought Nana. *A bundle of nerves. If he ever stopped talking long enough—what a wordy fellow he was—she would have to tell him about kickboxing. It really is a very good way to release one's tension.*

But truth be told, Officer Burly had good reason for holding the children's arms so tightly. You see, in addition to being frequent visitors to the Crispy County Police Department, Eufala and Bog were also frequent escapees.

Now it would be quite impossible to tell you every word of what Officer Burly had to say (there are not nearly enough pages left in this book), but to summarize the situation, it seems the children had been down at the park conducting an experiment involving a roller skate and a duck.

"Skateboard," corrected Bog.

In addition to the skateboard and the duck, a hill had been involved in the experiment, as were the noses of two people who had made two very unfortunate decisions about where to leap to avoid the speeding duck. There was also a woman sitting on a park bench, as well as a very large mud puddle, which apparently, as the children's experiment proved quite convincingly, could splash three feet in the air when hit at high speed by a skateboarding duck.

"Practically three and three-quarters," insisted Eufala.

It was all very fascinating. And thorough, too. Yes, the experiment sounded quite good to Nana.

Officer Burly, however, did not use the word
good. Or *fascinating*. In fact, from the many
words he did use, Nana was beginning to get the
impression that Officer Burly did not feel that
the experiment had gone very well at all.

"Perhaps," Nana began, but before she could
propose that the children give the experiment
another try, Officer Burly yanked the children

along with him. "All right, kids," he frowled
(no, there is no such word, but that did not stop
Officer Burly from frowling just the same), "let's
go call your mom."

10

Officer Not-So-Burly

Fortunately, the children were very good at thinking on their feet, which is why their causing-trouble-to-getting-in-trouble-for-it ratio was far superior to that of most other children their age.

In this case the solution was so simple that, really, it was hardly worth troubling their brains over at all.

"Nana can take us home," said Eufala.

"Yeah, Nana's our mom," said Bog, which was not at all what he meant to say. "I mean Nana's our mom's mom, so that makes her more than our mom, kind of like two moms, really, if you think about it—"

"Oh yes, yes, of course," said Nana just as Eufala was about to have to pinch some sense into her brother. "Come along then, children."

But Officer Burly did not look so eager to hand the children over to Nana. Not only that, but he seemed to be gripping the children's arms even more tightly than before.

"Hey! Letgomyarm!" said Bog.

"Now, Officer Burly, dear," said Nana, "if you ask me, you look a little feverish." (Officer Burly was, in fact, very red in the face.) "And there's that nerve condition of yours on top of it."

Nana had to stand on her tippy-toes in order to reach her hand high enough to feel Officer Burly's forehead.

"Yes, you are a bit warm, but don't you worry, a little rest on the couch and a nice cold Fudge Freezie will help you feel good as new."

Immediately after the words *Fudge* and *Freezie* were out of Nana's mouth, Officer Burly shrank. No, people do not just shrink, you are absolutely right, but something very similar to shrinking happened to Officer Burly. Even his voice got smaller. "My mama used to give me Fudge Freezies whenever I got owies," he said in a voice that sounded very much like a little boy's.

Eufala, feeling the itchiest kind of laugh coming on, immediately threw her free hand over Bog's mouth because as much as she wanted to laugh, she knew that Bog wanted to even more.

Their behavior did not go unnoticed by Officer Burly, however, who was not only back to his normal size, but back to his normal grumpiness as well. "Whenever I sustained an injury, that is," he said in a voice so deep he sounded just like a male siamang with strep throat—true, one does not often get to hear a male siamang with strep throat, but Nana, having worked as a zookeeper recently, was fortunate enough to have had the opportunity.

Officer Burly had by now released the children's arms and was far down the hall before Eufala and Bog let loose with all of their snorts and hoo-hees and belly slaps. They are very polite children, you see, and know that it is not courteous to laugh at people unless it is behind their backs.

Now something about that didn't sound quite right. Well, no matter, Nana had more important knots to untangle.

"Now then, just one little stop in the lab to solve a crime," said Nana, "and we'll be on our way."

While the children had no idea what Nana was talking about, they knew that it was bound to be interesting, because with Nana there was no such thing as not interesting. And so, exchanging giant bulging-eyeball looks as they went, they followed along behind Nana, who marched them down the hall and around the corner and directly through the door marked LAVATORY.

"How interesting," said Nana. "Now why, do you suppose, would they keep toilets in the lab?"

~~Hot Warm~~ Cold on the Trail of the Yumdum Thief

Once the children convinced Nana that they were not inside the lab but in fact inside the women's bathroom (such clever children) and after they had made a number of interesting pieces of artwork out of toilet paper (and so talented, too), the three set off in search of the lab.

"Bog, dear," said Nana as soon as they had made it through the correct door, "since you know so much about perfume, see what you can find out about this." She fished from her pocket a very precious looking pink bottle with *Eau de Toilette* written in loopy letters across it.

It was true that Bog knew a great deal about perfume. More specifically, his area of expertise had to do with what happens when perfume—his mother's to be precise—was mixed with various other things. A pot of spaghetti sauce, for example. The now brown-leafed fern on the windowsill, for instance. His homework—would Mr. Fleagal give him a better grade if his reports smelled like eau de toilette? And why was it called eau de toilette? Was there some reason? If he replaced his mother's eau de toilette with just plain toilette, would she notice? Much to Bog's surprise, no, she did not seem to notice at all. And so Bog did what any other bright but somewhat naughty child who was low on candy money would have done. He promptly replaced all three of his mother's bottles of eau de toilette with just plain toilette from the toilet bowl and sold the real stuff (renamed Eau de Bog) to the girls at school for a quarter a spritz.

Bog took the bottle of perfume from Nana's hand—a significantly less thrilling experience than swiping a bottle off his mother's dresser, but still, the bottle was not two seconds in his hand before his finger found the trigger and a great puff of perfume found a nearby microscope.

While Bog tested the perfume on various machinery and while Eufala read through Nana's notebook to catch herself up on the Yumdum case, Nana decided to place a few calls.

Now the phone at the Crispy County Police Department is not like an ordinary phone, nothing at all like the phone you might have on your kitchen counter, say. Imagine thirty phones glued together—that is approximately how many buttons are on the Crispy County Police Department phone. Nana had to push at least twenty of them just to find a dial tone.

"Now then," said Nana, punching in the phone number for Old McDonnelly.

Old McDonnelly had a farm, and on that farm he had some cows, and Nana thought perhaps he would have something to say about the half glass of wasted milk she had discovered in the O'Cleary house.

As Nana waited for Old McDonnelly to pick up, Eufala and Bog got familiar with the equipment available to them in the lab. Bog, who was by now out of perfume, continued his investigation by pouring the contents of every test tube he could find into Officer Burly's coffee mug to see if a colorful cloud of smoke would appear like the ones he had seen in his mad-scientist books.

Nothing. Not even a poof. Only a little light-headedness when he took a giant whiff of the stuff to see what it would smell like.

"Hello?" It was Old McDonnelly on the line, along with a *moo-moo* that Nana could hear so clearly she couldn't tell if it was a *moo-moo* here or a *moo-moo* there.

While Nana talked with Old McDonnelly, who was not at all happy to hear that his hard work and the hard work of his cows were going to waste, Eufala pulled out all of the mug shots she could find in the "Official Personnel Only" file cabinet and laid them out across the floor.

In addition to being a skilled artist, Eufala had developed a remarkable talent for altering photos (there were hundreds of old photos to be found in the trunk where her mother kept the family heirlooms). And so in order to better see what the thief might look like in various disguises, she gave a mustache to this one and sunglasses to that one. Some received buckteeth, others hairy ears. But all—because it was only fair—got to try on her Li'l Miss Precious® Frosted Cherry Lip Glitter™.

"There," she said, stepping back to admire her work.

"Yes, that is true," said Nana to Old McDonnelly, "quite right. If I were a cow, I would feel just the same way. Yes, I sure will, and you have a lovely day now, too."

"Well then," said Nana after she hung up the phone, "how about a little snack to celebrate? I'd say we're hot on the trail of this Yumdum thief."

Now, it did not seem to Eufala and Bog that they were hot on the trail of anything.

In fact, it did not seem that they had even located the correct trail or even the wilderness area in which the trail might be located.

But a little snack did sound nice.

"We could go to Happy's Candy Shop," suggested Bog.

"My thinking exactly," said Nana, who walked straight out the door without so much as her purse—which Bog grabbed off the coat rack—or her notebook—which Eufala plucked from the table.

12

The Perfect Trap

As always, Eufala and Bog headed straight for the bins of chewy candies while Nana hemmed and hawed her way down the chocolaty aisle.

While the children discussed the general merits and weaknesses of the various gummy products, Nana searched the shelves for something new to try. "Now these look very interesting," she mumbled to herself, as she scooped up a great pile of Yumdums.

Meanwhile, three aisles away, Bog—who was always at his most eloquent in the presence of sugar—was making a compelling argument in support of the gummy frog. "I mean, sure, the gummy cherry might have a well-balanced sweet and tarty taste, but the gummy frog has a far denser texture, which requires at least three times more chewing than the cherry and is therefore, of the two, a far better value. Of course, there's also—"

"Shhh," said Eufala, who all this time had been watching Nana teetering her way toward the checkout with Yumdums stacked up to her eyebrows.

"Well, it's true," said Bog, who was quite prepared to defend his case.

"No," whispered Eufala, "look over there."

From behind a giant vat of gummy bats, the children watched Nana set her Yumdums down on the counter.

"It's perfect," whispered Eufala.

"What's perfect?" said Bog.

"Shhh," said Eufala.

"What's perfect?" whispered Bog.

"A little old lady carrying a bunch of Yumdums," whispered Eufala. "It's the perfect trap."

"But Nana's not a little old lady," said Bog.

"Shhh," said Eufala.

"But Nana's not a little old lady," whispered Bog.

"Of course she isn't," whispered Eufala, "but the thief doesn't have to know that. Now put those frogs back and come help me."

13

Mmf Mmf Mmmfff

While it was not unusual for the children to grow rather serious in a candy shop—for the selection and purchase of candy, done correctly, requires enormous concentration and the application of years of experience—an even more serious kind of seriousness came over them now.

Sneaking up to the lollipop section and peering out from behind the giant swirlipops, they watched as Nana pulled two bills from her purse and laid them down on the counter. Then they watched as she gathered the Yumdums up again into a structure that looked remarkably like the Leaning Tower of Pisa.

The children quickly exchanged a few more whispers until it was agreed—or in this case it was Eufala telling Bog how it was going to be. They would wait a few minutes before leaving the shop, to give the thief time to make his move. He was far less likely to strike if they were with Nana.

And so when Nana hollered out, "Are you two dearies ready?" Eufala, almost too immediately, hollered back, "Almost! We'll catch up with you outside!" And Bog, almost too cluelessly,

hollered back, "Yeah, we want to watch what happens when mmf mmf mmmff—"

"When we mix gummy frogs with gummy bats," called Eufala, not moving her hand away from Bog's mouth until Nana was safely out of earshot.

"It wouldn't work," said Bog once he was in full control of his mouth again, "unless you melted them in a waffle iron or used a blow torch or something."

"Come on," said Eufala, "let's get to work."

A Lot Can Happen
in Two Pages After All

Outside the shop, Nana hobbled and wobbled under her leaning tower of Yumdums until the sweetest young boy, just the nicest young man, came along and offered to carry it for her. If only more young people were so courteous and kind.

"Well what a nice young man you are," said Nana. "You must be one of those Beagle Scouts." He was too old to be a Boy Scout and too young to be a marine. "You know, you really should earn a badge for this," said Nana. "I'll be sure to tell your captain first chance I get."

But oh my, was he hard to keep up with. He turned left and turned right and turned right and turned left and jumped bottles and puddles and poodles and bugles.

"Oh these—shoes," panted Nana, "are im-poss-ible!" And with a kick-kick she flipped off her shoes and dashed after that not-so-courteous young man who furthermore was not paying any attention to the crosswalk signals, which is not only against the law, but terribly unsafe.

Two Hundred and Ten Seconds Later

Now a candy shop is not the most ideal place to shop for thief-catching supplies, that is true, but a little creativity and a good understanding of candy physics can go a long way.

"You get the jawbreakers," said Eufala, "I'll get the licorice ropes."

But as they set off in search of their supplies, it seemed to each a shame to pass up so many perfectly good candies. So many perfectly delicious candies. So many perfectly within reach candies.

And so by the time they circled around the aisles and met up again at the counter, they had, between them, three jawbreakers, four licorice ropes, six packs of bubblegum, a bag of chocolate chummies, seven sour twisties, and two fistfuls of gummies.

"You never know," said Eufala, dropping her supplies down onto the counter, "what you might need."

"Yeah," said Bog, piling his selections on top of Eufala's, "it's not like we've ever caught a thief before."

"I mean," said Eufala, digging coins out from her pockets, "he could be dangerous."

"I know," said Bog, emptying his own pockets, "it's better to be sorry than safe."

"It's better to be *safe* than *sorry*," said Eufala.

"I already said that," said Bog.

"You said *sorry* than *safe*," said Eufala.

"What's the difference?" said Bog.

"There's a huge difference," said Eufala, "it's completely backward."

"Well what's so wrong with backward?" said Bog, who much preferred changing arguments to losing them.

While the children had made good time in gathering up their supplies, they had lost critical seconds in a completely pointless argument, not to mention Bog's dropping practically an entire gummy zoo on the floor (for a loss of twenty-three seconds), prompting Eufala to say, "Oh, great" (minus three seconds), and Bog to say, "It was an accident" (seven seconds). There was

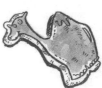

then the allegation at the checkout counter, put forth by Eufala, of a possible coin-counting fraud back at the fountain (for a total of forty-nine seconds), followed by the one-hundred-twenty-eight-second wait for one seemingly exhausted teenager to save his place in his comic book and slide his feet down off the counter so he could ring up their candies.

By the time the children managed to get themselves and their thirty-eight thief-catching supplies out the door, Nana, as you might have guessed by now, was nowhere to be seen.

Bagel Scout's Honor

With licorice ropes flung over their shoulders and gummies stuffed into their cheeks, the children stood outside the shop and argued about which way Nana might have gone.

"Viff vay," said Eufala, gnawing on a gummy frog (and proving Bog's theory that the frog truly was the most resilient gummy).

"Viff vay," said Bog, pointing in the opposite direction.

"Bofe," said Eufala, and so it was agreed that they would check both directions.

After neither direction produced a nana, not even a trace of a nana, the children took to racing up and down and around the streets like…well, for lack of a more poetic description, like two children in search of their missing grandmother, who was, by now, quite likely being chased after by a wanted, and very possibly dangerous, thief.

When they finally caught up with Nana, she was two blocks away, sitting on the sidewalk beside a very tired-looking boy. The boy was nodding as Nana patted his knee. "Now the red hand," said Nana, "that means stop."

At first the children's only concern was seeing Nana patting that boy's knee—like he was one of her grandchildren—which he was *not*.

But then they saw, half-hidden under the boy's shirt and stuffed into both socks— Yumdums!

"Nana! You caught him! You caught the Yumdum thief!" shouted Eufala, grabbing the licorice ropes from her shoulders and preparing to make a lunge at the boy's ankles.

"Get him get him get him!" shouted Bog, holding a giant jawbreaker out in front of him in case the thief should make a move to escape.

"Oh now, you sillies," said Nana, "this is Henry. Henry is a Beagle Scout."

"But look!" squeaked Eufala, pointing to the Yumdums stuffed up under Henry's shirt. "He stole your Yumdums!"

"Oh my," said Nana with a giggle. "Beagle Scouts don't steal. Isn't that right, Henry?"

and she gave the boy the kind of smile that the children felt very certain belonged to them. In fact, to Eufala and Bog, the boy getting one of Nana's smiles felt like an even worse kind of thievery than stealing a bunch of worthless old Yumdums.

As for Henry, Nana's smile got to him as well. Henry, you see, had been called a lot of things in his life (not such good things, in truth), but never before had he ever been called a Beagle Scout. And though he had no idea what a Beagle Scout was (in fact, what Henry had heard was Bagel Scout, which only added to the appeal, especially if there was to be some cream cheese and grape jelly to go along with it), he now wanted nothing more than to be the best Bagel Scout ever in the history of Bagel Scouts.

But since he was not yet a Bagel Scout and since he imagined that lying was not something a Bagel Scout did either, all he could think to do was cry.

"There, there," said Nana, patting the boy on his knee. "You've had a very hard day, haven't you, Henry dear?"

Henry sniffled and nodded in a way that made Bog want to kick him in the shin.

"Now I want you to march straight home," said Nana, "and get yourself a nice cold Fudge Freezie."

Henry sniffled and nodded some more. And then, to the shock and horror of Eufala and Bog, he stood up and began to walk away, Yumdums dropping out from his shirt and socks with every step.

Well, you can imagine the look on the children's faces. If you are having trouble imagining, you must only picture two large black circles—those would be their mouths, which were opened wider than mouths were ever meant to be opened (really, you mustn't try this at home).

As they watched the boy walking in one

direction and Nana walking in the other, Eufala and Bog didn't know which way to run first.

"He's escaping!" screeched Eufala, leaping toward the thief.

"You're supposed to send him to jail," demanded Bog, making a grab for Nana's sleeve.

But it was no use. In fact, Henry had already disappeared around a corner, and Nana had already turned and begun walking home. At first the children were unable to move. They could only stare.

How could she have just let him go like that?

"It's not fair," said Bog.

Of course the last thing they wanted to do right then was follow after Nana, but eventually they did, making sure to lift their knees high and bring their feet down hard so there would be no mistaking their position on the matter.

"Well now," said Nana once the children were

beside her, "I don't imagine our Henry will be stealing again for a very long time."

"You knew?" said Eufala.

"But you said—" started Bog.

Nana didn't answer, she only smiled and said, "Now which one of you detectives is going to give me a ride?"

Goodness, What Well-Behaved Children

"Nana, you have to hold on tighter," insisted Eufala, who was getting a bit tired of having to go back for Nana every time she got bounced off the skateboard.

"Yes, yes," said Nana with a giggle that sounded suspiciously like someone who enjoyed getting bounced off the back of a skateboard.

When they arrived back home, Nana stood in the yard and watched as Eufala boosted Bog up to the kitchen window. Then she watched as Bog hung a dish towel out the window so Eufala could grab hold and hoist herself up.

She did not ask the children why they were climbing through the window, but then it was not her habit to ask why. Anyway, it seemed like perfectly good fun to her.

And so she just smiled and waved. Waved and smiled.

Smiled and waved.

"Mother, why on earth are you waving at our kitchen window?"

Nana did not have to turn around to know who it was. Or to know what look would be on the face of who it was. In fact, perhaps it was best that she not turn around at all.

"Oh, I'm just waving to Eufala and Bog," Nana said in the most cheerful of voices. "It's been such a lovely afternoon."

Elaine, who believed this to mean that Nana had spent the entire afternoon waving at the kitchen window, immediately took to chewing on the inside of her cheek. Waving at the kitchen window all afternoon, can you

imagine? It was at times like this that Elaine felt most strongly that Nana really did belong in the nursing home, where someone could look after her.

"Well, why on earth," said Elaine, "didn't you just go inside?"

And then she remembered. She had told the children to never open the front door.

What wonderfully well-behaved children.

As Elaine stood beside Nana, waving up at her two wonderfully well-behaved children—oh the pride, the indescribable pride—she had the most unnatural urge, a reckless thought really, that perhaps just this once she would allow the children one small piece of candy—provided, of course, that they eat every bite of their Swiss chard. And—this goes without saying—that they floss and brush their teeth directly afterward.

HELP WANTED

BACKHOE OPERATOR

MUST NOT DROP DIRT WHERE DIRT IS NOT NEEDED.

BERRY PICKER

MUST KNOW YOUR BLACKBERRIES FROM YOUR SPLATBERRIES, YOUR STRAWBERRIES FROM YOUR SLOPBERRIES, YOUR BOYSENBERRIES FROM YOUR POISONBERRIES.

BURGER FLIPPER

GOOD AT TENNIS? BADMINTON YOUR SPORT? YOU COULD BE A NATURAL!

DENTIST

TO SCRAPE PLAQUE FROM TEETH AND DIG BACTERIAL BUILDUP FROM GUMS.

ELF

WILL CONSIDER VERY SMALL PERSONS WITH POINTY EARS AND GOOD BUILDING SKILLS.

GYMNASTICS TEACHER

NEEDED TO BEND AND TWIST CHILDREN INTO VARIOUS SHAPES.

HERO

POPULARITY AWAITS YOU IN THIS EXCITING CAREER AS A VILLAIN-FIGHTING SPECIALIST. MUST PROVIDE OWN CAPE.

LION TAMER

WITH LESS DELICIOUS-LOOKING HEAD TO REPLACE PREVIOUS LION TAMER.

MECHANIC

NEEDED: EXPERT IN RATTLES, SHIMMERS, CLANGS, KABONGS, PEETERS, PUTTERS, AND ZBONGS!

MIND READER

I'M THINKING OF AN ADDRESS WHERE YOU SHOULD SEND YOUR RESUME.

MOTHER

WHO DOESN'T BARK AT ME ALL DAY TO CLEAN MY ROOM AND BRUSH MY TEETH AND PUT ON MY SHOES.